Table of Contents

Fusion *(noun)*

2a. a merging of diverse, distinct, or separate elements into a unified whole.

Acknowledgments:

Thanks to each and every single one of our amazing students whose contributions made this piece possible. While we could not accept every single entry, there were so many wonderful ones that explored the theme in new and interesting ways. The skill and diversity of not just the stories, but perspectives, has really made this into something that we are all so proud of. Thanks also to our judges, Lili Pâquet and Ariella Van Luyn for their advice and hard work judging the entries.

<u>Contributors:</u>

Henry E. C. Grant

Kelly Jones 琼斯凯莉 / 蔡亹平 Cai Menping

Tashi Dema

Lynn Stahlhut

Anonymous

Ruvinda de Mel

Mel Kennard

Rick Slater

Bethany Eickhoff

Sayed Ahmed

Introduction

By Ash Taylor

When we first started brainstorming this project, we wanted it to be something that would last, something that students could contribute to that wouldn't just be a Student Magazine (not to say, of course, that student magazines aren't important). Our goal has always been to provide our students with valuable experiences relevant to their degree and chosen career fields. What initially began as a single idea – a student focused publication – soon became larger, and more ambitious. Other universities have literary journals, regular publications, student magazines. Why not us?

Since its inception, UNE has been a pioneer. From the very beginning UNE has offered distance education; first through correspondence, and now online. This has allowed thousands of students across Australia to pursue a university education – an opportunity that without the ability to study from home, they might not have had the chance for otherwise. This, together with TuneFM's birth as an intersection of science and music, led us to developing a theme that we felt encapsulated all the multitudes that make up not just our students, but also our history.

What better way to celebrate and honour this history of hybridity than through the theme of Fusion? For most people, fusion calls to mind nuclear plants, or the extreme heat of a star's internal mechanics. When you really look at it, when you look at the other definitions of the word, that's when you begin to see it in another light. At its core, fusion is an act of creation – it's the coming together of cultures, the act of trying something new. It's not just limited to science and physics, but present in our every-day life, and the works published in this anthology reflect that.

From hardboiled tech-noir detectives hunting down impossible AI, to the thoughtful exploration of your own identity as a biracial person, there are so many possibilities and interpretations of a simple word that you might never have dreamed of. The quality of works that our contributors have produced is impeccable; each and every one brings their own unique perspective to the world, and the theme. Within the pages of this publication, you'll find a range of very different stories, but each one is still connected by this central theme.

In a way, this anthology is a fusion itself – it's a creation borne from separate individuals, coming together to create a unified body of work.

To share in the act of creation is a wonderful thing.

About the Cover

By Henry E. C. Grant

For this piece I assembled photographs of nature I had previously taken (a sea-dragon, the ocean, the sky, a tree etc.) and digitally edited the images together. I wanted to represent the theme of fusion primarily through the contrast between the natural subjects of the photographs and the digital medium. The distorted artwork makes these natural forms seem almost artificial, and it's difficult to tell where one object ends. and another begins - as if the different elements have fused together.

I also wanted to portray a contrast in both the saturation and value of colour - the artwork uses a lot of contrast between black and white, and monochrome and bright colours. However, despite the contrast in colours, there are many areas of grey and I wanted to portray an effect that appeared as if all the different colours in the image were seeping into each other and mixing to relate back to the overarching theme of fusion. Additionally, given it is currently Pride Month,[1] I thought it made sense to use a spectrum of bright colours in my artwork, with the colours surrounding the artwork reminiscent of pride flags - representing a community that is a fusion of many different people.

---

[1] The piece was submitted/created during pride month

The typography of the word fusion is depicted once in legible text for readability, and then in a mirrored effect using different fonts for each letter - this text instead looks like a wild fusion. Essentially, for this cover art I wanted to create something chaotic, bold and colourful, while clearly depicting the theme of fusion - a fusion of nature and technology, a fusion of light and dark, and a fusion of colour and monochrome. I wanted my artwork to appear interesting and mysterious in a way where it could be interpreted differently by each person.

In a sense, each person is kind of a fusion themselves - a mix of their life experiences and the people they've met.

Ching Chong

By Kelly Jones 琼斯凯莉 / 蔡亹平 Cai Menping

Content warning: Domestic violence, racism.

The fusion of A and Bis ... AB or C? When C exists, A and B have vanished, like the parents of the *Graveyard of the Fireflies* children, but C's existence is a linear consequence of A and B. By contrast, AB is still living at home, either a filial child subservient to A and/or B, or maybe rebelling at home. Is a mixed-race child's culture the fusion of AB or the fusion of C?

Until recently, I insisted that I was an AB fusion. I really believed there was no such thing as A vs. B. I'm a 3rd-gen Cantonese, 9th-gen mongrel descendant from a Staffordshire convict called Elizabeth Whitmore, and I believed that there was no such thing as East or West, either culturally or geographically. I'm an integrated whole, thus, where is that boundary? Is my sense of smell more Cantonese than Anglo? Is Russia East, Near East, Near-Middle East, Far East or Near West? How adventitious these divisions are. They're merely cultural conventions. Like Lao Tzu would say: black creates white, tall creates short, in creates out.

But I was brought up in rural white Australia (Northern Tablelands NSW), speaking English, eating vegemite on toast, sausages and mash, bread and butter puddings, going to church on

Sundays, and attending schools where the popular kids were blonde-haired and blue-eyed. My siblings and I were the only Chinese students at one rural NSW school, except for a boy that was literally called "Chinese Takeaway" by the other school kids. This was in the 1980's.

Natives of Guangdong 广东 My great-aunt, great-great-grandmother, and great-grandmother (mother's father's mother). Early 1900s.

In Sydney, I had two full-blood Cantonese cousins, and their mother spoke fluent Cantonese. When I visited my very short, stout grandmother *(d. 2009)* in Strathfield, Sydney, she would swing with me down to the shops, rowing both walking canes like she was skiing along the pavement. In central Strathfield I would hear her happily chatter to shopkeepers in Cantonese, proudly showing off her grandchild.

My great-grandmother (mother's mother's mother) with three of her four children in Burwood, Sydney. 1930s.

In the 1950's, she had separated from her husband and raised her two children single-handedly, while also working as a secretary. The White Australia policy had a very strong impact on their lives. My mother, her only daughter, didn't learn much Cantonese: she could count to ten, knew the names of lots of different foods and her mother would tell her to " xǐshǒu" (洗手 *wash your hands* - I've written the Mandarin as it sounds very similar). My mother mostly spoke English at home, went to Central Baptist in the CBD, and they never visited Daoist temples anymore.

My mother, me as a baby, my older brother, father, and older sister in Corowa, NSW. Note the blue shearer's singlet and Tonka truck. 1970s.

My father and mother did their first Acts of Fusion in their very early 20s (way too early), largely because my Nan Jones said, "Beverly would make a very good mother". She did, too.

My father was anti-Chinese. She was a timid, myopic wife, and when he smashed her glasses on her face, she rang Lifeline for help, who told her she "was a doormat" and should leave. But she stayed with her Aussie Battler, whose parenting and animal husbandry relied on fear and violence, not only whipping livestock until they were bloody and trembling, or shooting a "bad tempered" animal, but also whipping the children and punching the wife. Talking back was dangerous. My mother assimilated very rapidly.

This method of fusing had many consequences. I was a very shy being. When I was in seventh grade in high school, I was given the role of "Ying Poo" the Chinaman, in the school play. I had a long black plait and spoke in a silly sing-song voice; I thought it was perfectly natural. During rehearsal one Saturday afternoon, I was too frightened to ask where the girl's toilets were, and when going on stage for my part, my bladder burst and I ran off into the wings and the urine ran down my legs, flooding across the timber floorboards. It was terribly humiliating.

When I was about 16, after church one Sunday, I wished to say something about the sermon because I dared to disagree with the pastor. My father's response was, "You can leave home immediately!" No talking back included not voicing any dissenting opinion. Fundamentalist Protestantism taught me that God would strike me from heaven with some terrible punishment if I were disobedient and sinful. When I left the church at the age of 19, in my second year of uni, I was still arguing mentally with an imaginary God and genuinely feared that I'd cop an awful supernatural punishment. It took quite a while to stop feeling like a guilty evildoer.

Wiping out the B made me believe there was no such thing as East and West, let alone East vs. West. "Look at me! I'm Eastern and Western, so they aren't mutually exclusive." I said stuff like that then. I didn't realise there was no B in my life.

Compartmentalising helped keep the fiction going. Sometimes, I realised that there was a massive, ancient culture out there, off-bounds, because I couldn't understand even a single Chinese language. I knew some version of "你好吗 nǐ hǎo ma" (how are you) and "我很高兴认识你 wǒ hěn gāoxìng rènshí nǐ" (I'm pleased to meet you) because when I was 20, in my third year at Sydney University, I started an Adult Education course, but it was too hard to keep up. I visited Chinese suburbs, saw lots of unreadable Chinese advertising, hankered after foods in Chinese grocery shops that I couldn't read the labels of. So much existed that I was ignorant of. But I still maintained, I was AB.

Enter COVID-19 in March 2020. My father decided it was a Chinese conspiracy to start and win WW3, parroting a list of reasons copied from Facebook. I think I saw red! I replied in an equally-bloody-minded way, listing dot points on why that was incredibly dumb idea. Is the Chinese government so stupid as to vandalise their economy and social cohesion? Or are they extreme masochists?

Like the craven bully he really is, he ran away and would not dare speak to me. We have been estranged since then. I certainly don't invite dialogue as I see him as a perpetrator of domestic violence and racist abuse against my mother, siblings and myself. I think he should have done jail time. He threw a hammer at my younger brother's head, narrowly avoiding killing him. Although my three siblings (most of their children have blue eyes, some even have blonde hair) say there's no point in challenging him, as "he's never going to change/ he's too old / he'll never apologise", I continue on my path because I believe silence is compliance.

In late 2020, chewing over the disturbed feelings about my lost Chinese-ness, I flipped the bird and decided to start learning Mandarin Chinese. The University of Tasmania offered an online Diploma of Languages, and I studied that part-time, switching to UNE 's Diploma of Modern Languages in 2022 for smaller tutorial classes – thankfully, it was a very good decision! I've now been studying Chinese for almost four years and know 5700+ words.

Last year, I went to China for the first time – alone! Every language student wants to test their skills in a native environment. The food was mostly very confusing. I got ripped off a few times as I don't have that essential native Chinese skill of bargaining. That's when it really hit me: the division between East and West really does exist. It's not originally or innately political. That's a consequence. As a side note, Australia has a strong political boundary drawn against China because of Australia's political alliance with the US. The US and China are basically the two biggest political powers in the world. Because Australia's culture is predominantly Western, it follows West-centric policies, while desperately trying to maintain peaceful relations with China, to maintain trade and economic stability.

While in China, I noticed things like:

- Drivers changed lanes without waiting for a space to move into, yet there were no accidents
- Roadworks were terribly haphazard and lacked safety warnings or barriers, yet drivers seemed to have an amazing ability to adjust to their immediate surroundings
- Chinese people I spent time with trusted the government, and showed pride and contentment rather than fear, anger and uneasiness as one would expect if living in a corrupt and authoritarian regime
- Most people were slim, fit, active and down-to-earth
- I rarely saw women wearing dresses or getting all fancied up, even in central Shanghai (except in the Bund)
- The working hours were very long (e.g. the post office was open on Sundays from 7am to 9pm)
- Cities were very clean, and cleaners were ubiquitous. There were no big machines and high tech; manual labour was predominant
- Asking someone if they've eaten as a *greeting* makes sense when everyone is so slim and works so hard; it's about helping each other be productive

- Western fashions and behaviours are very trendy, yet most Chinese people I met couldn't speak English to save themselves, even at major city transport hub help desks!

I got the very strong sense that Chinese mainlanders are a united family. I felt safe, as though strangers were relatives. The fact that I got ripped off several times made me realise that, yes, I could belong to that family, but only if I learnt how the rules worked. With hundreds of years of Confucianism, which emphasises family, filial piety and social cohesion, and decades of single-child families creating strong bonds between unrelated children, that solidarity makes sense.

These are just my personal thoughts. China is not "home", but nor is Australia "home". I know how the rules work here in Australia as a "native" white, but I still feel bereft of part of my heritage. I'm 50% Southern Chinese by DNA but Cantonese culture and language are both very unfamiliar. Plus, I hate the humidity! But I loved how no one in China who met me asked me what country I was from. Many people said they thought I was Chinese.

Fusion? Biologically, yes, fusion is a reality, like yellow and blue seamlessly blending to make green. But culturally, it's like me ordering sweet and sour pork at a Chinese takeaway at some Aussie town. I can't stand it. I take it home, rinse off the MSG-laden sauce, pick off all the batter, add lots of yummy broccoli-green gailaan, 木耳 (mu er, literally, *wood ear,* a wavy black-brown fungus), and lots of other chop-chop veggies. For most of my life, this East-West fusion dish was not AB, but *Ab.* I would now say that I taste more like a C. So, I'm **AbC.** 哈哈哈！(Hahaha!)

Left: *Me, a freckled AbC..* ***Right****: My beautiful, happy, creative, and playful mother at Tantanoola Caves, SA*

About the Author:

Ah dear, how do I write 100 words about myself for this anthology? I can string a pile of tags together like a Google newsfeedbot; but am I the whole string of those tags? Let's just say, I am a "what" rather than a "who": a nanofizz in causality, changing every instant, a swirling micro-eddy in the strange river of this unspeakably immense universe. My brain says I'm real, tangible, someone people like to smile at, but I feel a lot of ambiguity and anxiety.

Digital Blessings

By Tashi Dema

The cold autumn day of April 19, 2022, was the day faith, culture and technology converged. It was a tryst of faith and resilience. It was the day social media bridged all physical distance and provided comfort in distress.

My three-year-old daughter was crying inconsolably on her father's back when I returned home from the university. My husband told me she fell off the trampoline. When I took her to the hospital, the doctors said she had a knee fracture, and they immobilised her leg with a cast to keep the fractured bones in place and ensure proper healing.

With Armidale facing acute shortage of medical practitioners (Murphy, 2023), the wait at the emergency department of Armidale Hospital was long. During our six hours wait before we could see a doctor, I called my cousin brother, who is a senior monk in a monastery back home in Bhutan, a tiny Himalayan country.

As is the practice of most Bhutanese families whenever someone fell ill, I asked my brother to consult a local religious masters and astrologers to find out why the misfortune fell on my daughter. I sent him about $400 AUD to conduct the rituals.

My cousin brother visited two important monasteries that evening (which was afternoon in Bhutan, as Bhutan is four hours behind Armidale). He first visited Kurjey Lhakhang, where the great Indian Saint Padma Sambhava, who is also popularly known as Guru Rinpoche in Buddhism, subdued a wrathful local deity in the eighth century. He then visited Jambay Lhakhang, one of the 108 temples built by a Tibetan king Songtsen Gompo in a day, in the seventh century. He consulted the religious masters and astrologers and asked the monks in the two monasteries to conduct rituals. He made the offerings on our behalf.

My cousin sent me videos when the rituals were conducted so that I could make my prayers on the social media app, WeChat. I not only prayed while watching the videos, but also put the phone on my daughter's head while I said the most sincere prayers every time I watched the videos.

Culture, indigenous beliefs and practices

Bhutanese people believe in the adage that medical consultation and ritualistic practices should be done together whenever someone falls ill. Bhutanese people, who are mostly Buddhist, also rely heavily on rituals and prayers to heal. From cleansing ceremonies right after the birth of a child to after death rituals, Bhutanese people perform many kinds of rituals. There are annual rituals, popularly known as 'lochoe', rituals conducted for the sick, rituals to dispel misfortune, rituals to ward off evils and bring in luck, peace and happiness. Rituals are conducted on important occasions like venturing into business or making a long journey. They are simply countless.

A French ethno-historian and Tibetologist, Francoise Pommaret, who studied Bhutanese culture extensively, claimed that Buddhist concepts shape the thoughts and life of the people. Religious ceremonies are performed on official occasions, and grand religious festivals and rituals are sponsored by the state.

In her work, 'Bon and chos – community rituals in Bhutan', Pommaret explains that Buddhism in the Himalayas incorporated the local deities, numina, who reside in rivers, rocks, forests, mountains, and makes them part of an extensive pantheon. "The worship of these local deities through appropriate rituals constitute an essential part of the religious life of the Bhutanese," the study stated[2].

A study on the health system found that a large body of research in the west and Asia has found that most people pray or perform rituals during their illness and hospitalization in order to cope with serious adversity[3].

---

[2] Pommaret, Francoise. (2006). *Bon and chos, community rituals in Bhutan.*
[3] Pelzang, Rinchen. (2010). *Religious practice of the patients and families during illness and hospitalization in Bhutan.* Journal of Bhutan Studies. 22. 77-97.

Most rituals are conducted to appease local deities to invoke blessings and seek protection. As a daughter of a local bon practitioner in a remote village, I grew up believing my father's rituals brought the rain during paddy cultivation season and good weather during paddy harvest time. A person from every household in the village of 20 households would gather in our house with flour, rice, meat, butter and cheese to help my father conduct the rituals. Villagers would consult my father if someone in their family or cattle fell sick. My father would pull his beads to find out what caused the sickness and then advise the family to conduct rituals. He would do simple rituals like alcohol libation and smoke cleansing. The family would conduct rituals with the help of Buddhist monks and layman if the illness was serious.

The power of belief and prayers

Bhutanese people believe in the power of prayers and rituals. There is no explanation to the mystic belief, but it helps many navigate their daily mundane life and its happenings. There are numerous lived experiences of patients recovering after their families conducted rituals, even after the medical practitioners gave up on them.

When a colleague shared a harrowing experience of her son's accident in Sydney to a member of the Bhutanese community in

Armidale, Pema, and how the doctors had given up, Pema asked her friends in Bhutan to conduct rituals. "I sent money and the religious masters in Bhutan said the boy will get better," Pema said. The religious master conducted prayers virtually and the boy showed progress. He can now walk. "I don't know how to explain it, but my friend has believed in prayers since that time," Pema said.

Prayers and rituals in times of sickness and misfortune is a part of Bhutanese culture. Many people have deep spiritual connections to these beliefs and traditions. Seeking solace in divine intervention in times of need is a part of Bhutan's cultural identity. The practice is deeply ingrained in the ways of life and gets passed down through generations inherently. When I shared the news of a Bhutanese community member's airlift to Newcastle recently, after she had some lung complication, my 12-year-old daughter took her four-year-old sister to pray for the patient in our small altar. They closed their eyes, folded their hands and mumbled some mantras.

A Bhutanese academician, who is also a popular documentary filmmaker and communication specialist, Dorji Wangchuk, recounted many stories of how his close associates, who live in the United States of America and were diagnosed with terminally ill diseases like cancer, recovered after conducting rituals and prayers in Bhutan.[4] He explained that magic, mysticisms and miracles happen in the mountains of Bhutan even as modernisation takes over.[5]

An article in one of India's newspapers, The Statesman, describes Bhutan as a country with spiritual practices and beliefs interwoven into the very fabric of its society. "For centuries, the kingdom has been a sanctuary for Buddhist practitioners, and it continues to be a place where religion thrives," the article stated. "Bhutan's spiritual heritage and the country's Buddhist traditions make it a unique and special place."[6]

Even as modernity and globalisation grip the country, Bhutan's spiritual heritage is a testament to the power and influence of Buddhism in the country. The teachings and traditions of this ancient religion have shaped the culture, traditions, and values of the Bhutanese people for centuries.

Bhutanese diaspora and virtual blessings

As a small country with a population of about 770,000 people,[7]

---

[4] Wangchuk, Dorji. (2023). *"Of Rituals and Recoveries."* Dorji Wangchuk.
[5] Wangchuk, Dorji. (2022) *"Power of Prayers and Faith."* Dorji Wangchuk.
[6] Ani. (2023) *"Exploring Bhutan's Spiritual Heritage, Buddhist Traditions."* The Statesman.
[7] Choden, Y., Admin and Zangmo, S. (2024) *National Statistics Bureau; Population (Projected),* National Statistics Bureau.

migration has been identified as a pressing issue for Bhutan. About 64,000 Bhutanese have migrated outside in the last few years, making about nine percent of the population. [8]Nearly 30 percent of the diaspora are below 35 years.

Many media outlets, Bhutanese and international, cited stagnant economy in the country and exploring economic opportunities as the main cause of migration. Many migrants claim seeking economic stability as their main reason for migrating. Youth unemployment at its highest at 22.4 percent. An article by ABC claimed Bhutan confronts an existential challenge[9]. Bhutan's Prime Minister, Tshering Tobgay, acknowledged that migration poses an existential threat in the country in his first 'State of the nation' report earlier this year[10]. He came to power after winning election in January this year.

While the Bhutanese diaspora live across the world and integrate into new societies, they always preserve their tradition and culture and social media platforms are helping the diaspora stay connected with their families back home, participate in spiritual and ritualistic practices. Many families in Bhutan share

---

[8] Dolkar, Dechen. (2024) *"Migration poses an existential threat: PM."* Kuensel Online.

[9] Dias, A. and Patidar, S. (2023) *'it feels so empty': The Forbidden Kingdom of Bhutan is turning into a ghost town,* ABC News.

[10] Editor (2024) *Prime minister presents the state of the nation report to the Joint Sitting of Parliament,* National Assembly of Bhutan.

rituals conducted in their homes and community to their family members abroad. Many times, rituals are live streamed so that diaspora could virtually participate. Such sharing of the blessings digitally blends traditional practices with opportunities of digital technology. There are also virtual consultations with lamas and shamans on an everyday basis.

Fear/Love

By Lynn Stahlhut

Content warning: Domestic violence

I*t is a hot afternoon, oppressively hot in the way that only the days of one's childhood may be. We run through the house, laughing, chasing each other around ringed lounges, through the kitchen while Mum laughs. Tiny legs launch hot potato feet from the burning concrete stairs, leaping onto the cool of the green lawn and scrambling to avoid our small sister gleefully aiming a squirting hose in our direction.*

We didn't hear the car, this time.

"Dad's home." Mum is scooping up my sister with her right arm, turning off the hose with her left. A broken left arm, her dominant side, years earlier had forced her to become ambidextrous.

My older brother is shivering slightly, his ribs showing through his puckered skin. Mum slings a towel from the clothesline and tosses it to him while carrying my sister inside. We follow like anxious ducklings.

"Who left the fucking front door open again?" The house is tiny, and the slamming of the front door rattles everything inside it.

"Letting all the heat in." He kicks off his shoes and sits heavily on his lounge.

"What's this shit?" he mutters as he turns off whatever childish nonsense we had been watching.

"And who left the fucking back door open too? Stupid." He shouts over his shoulder but doesn't turn to receive a reply. Clustered around the loungeroom door, we are silent.

"You want a cup of tea, hun?" Mum asks soothingly. He grudgingly agrees as he flicks through the channels.

My tiny sister is now clinging to my oldest brother, who is drying her with his towel.

My other brother leaves through the back door, slamming it as he exits. Mum and I wince at the bellowed expletives that follow for whoever slammed the fucking door so hard.

I first read *Jane Eyre* when I was a teen. I was told it was simply a "grown up version of *Pride and Prejudice*", but I found nothing similar between my favourite book and this monstrosity. I didn't know then why I had such an adverse reaction, I was furious that people worldwide had called this the beginning of romance, a feminist triumph, a love for the ages, while it left me with only a greasy, angry feeling in my stomach.

"I don't love your mother," my dad tells me.

I am not yet a teen. Tears well in my eyes. My sister has already hidden, weeping. I don't recall where my brothers were.

There is a smash as he finishes another beer and misses the bin with his off-hand toss.

"I don't love your mother," he repeats. "But I worry about her."

I try to hide my now-streaming face. He doesn't notice anyway.

"I don't love her because she doesn't love me."

He nods into my shocked face, "You ask her, she doesn't love me. You ask her. I don't love her. But I worry about her."

He mutters on like this for another few hours, mutters about love and worry, and mutters about pregnancy being a trap to marry the unloved man.

Why would anyone want to marry my dad?

My Mum arrives home a little later than anticipated. She pales as she sees what she is walking into, strewn bottles, little red faces, one big angry baby.

Later she soothes my sobs as I repeat the hurtful things he has said. "He's just drunk." She strokes my hair.

"It's my fault for not coming home sooner."

I have wondered often why it is that so many women become trapped in these nightmares of coercive control, these abusers who are excused for their lack of overt violence. Obsessed, as I am, with stories in all forms, I turn to literature to find an understanding of this behaviour, of the acceptability of captivity and violence in romance.

In my early twenties I read the *Twilight* saga. My friends were obsessed with the books. They were an easy read but sat uneasily in my stomach. I recall a scene in which the protagonist, Bella, attempts to visit her werewolf friends. Her car won't start. Her boyfriend, the vampire Edward, steps forth from the shadows. He has been watching her and has realised her intended course of action. He cannot allow her to visit with werewolves. For her own protection. So, he has disabled her vehicle.

Bella vents her frustration, but Edward only looks morose and tells her to close her window if she does not wish to see him that night. Furious, Bella charges upstairs and slams shut her bedroom window, and my younger self cheered.

Then she reopens it. A greasy, angry feeling settled over me. Some people find this book romantic. Some people find these actions romantic.

Rosie Waterland had a similar experience watching the *50 Shades of Grey* movies. The Australian author wrote two bestselling autobiographies detailing her violent childhood with humour and honesty. She told her fans to follow along as she live-tweeted the fun sexy romp that the movie was billed as. She lasted maybe 20 minutes before tweeting that this was not fun. This was not romance. This was abuse.[11]

When I am preparing to move to college, my Dad sits me down to talk about budgeting. He breaks down income and expenditures in a simple fashion, writing the numbers in columns on a piece of paper. I nod along, pleasing him with my alacrity. We both find the logic in numbers and patterns easy to understand.

"Your mother has to put hers in little yellow envelopes, so she doesn't spend too much."

He explains, "Because she's stupid with money."

I tense and remain silent.

"I'm not good with money." Mum agrees.

Returning to *Jane Eyre* as an adult, my youthful disturbance returned but now I had the context to understand why. Rochester's behaviour towards Jane is possessive, obsessive, and controlling.

[11] Waterland, R. (2015) *Rosie Reviews: Fifty Shades of Grey.* https://www.mamamia.com.au/fifty-shades-of-grey-review-rosie-waterland/

Once again, I am baffled that this is considered a love story, and I am not alone in this opinion. While my teenage self did not have the words to describe Rochester's behaviour, my adult self has the benefit not only of introspective hindsight but recent studies and legislation around a newly named form of abuse: Coercive Control. This is violence without *violence*, recently reclaimed as abuse, even if "he didn't hit me."

Much like my child-self asked why anyone would want to marry my Dad, I seek to answer the question why anyone would want to marry Mr Rochester? How did this socially acceptable obsessive control become codified as romantic rather than abusive? Why was Mr Darcy's love of Elizabeth acceptable in Pride and Prejudice, while Rochester's similarly devoted attachment terrifying for me?

I am visiting my parents over Christmas. I am navigating a very painful divorce - poorly. I am not well equipped to deal with conflict.

I sit outside in the shade with my Dad and my brothers. They are companionably drinking beers. I can't stand the smell. I am silently running through topics in my head, trying to find something to discuss that won't set anyone off.

Not even the weather.

"It's too fucking hot in there." Dad growls.

"Your fucking mother opened all the doors and let the cool air out, the stupid bitch."

My brothers stare at their beers and say nothing.

I stand abruptly, "Don't call my Mum that!"

I retreat to my room in the garage to cry.

My brother calls goodbye as he leaves.

Later, my Mum and I talk as we take a long walk. I understand now why we took so many long walks as kids. "You know he's just stressed because of your divorce." She's trying to manage my emotions as well.

I shake my head, "Do you know what he said?"

She doesn't, she was just told there was a disagreement. I suppose my brothers tried to shield her. She assumes he has said something slighting to me about my failure.

"He called you a stupid bitch." I almost choke on the words.

She freezes for a second, and then attempts to strangle me with hugs. She knows I am not the cuddly type, but she is beside herself. She weeps into my shoulder, my tiny Mummy, and I wonder if it is the first time anyone has stood up for her against my bear of a father.

In *Jane Eyre* we trace the journey of the orphaned waif Jane from her difficult childhood to governess of the mysterious stately home of Thornfield. We are terrified of the mysterious, ghostly presence she finds there, and watch helpless as this guileless, ignorant virgin marries an older, sexually charged man who has locked his mad wife in his attic. *Jane Eyre* is a child of the Gothic genre, and her hero Rochester is likewise. Gothic Horror as a genre has been influenced by grisly folktales like Bluebeard, and the horror tales of the 18th century. Authors use the language of such influential texts as *MacBeth* and *Paradise Lost* to create narratives of satanic terror and macabre thrills.[12]

Through the intermingling of Gothic with Romance in *Jane Eyre*, the dark Gothic Villain became fused with the romantic hero. Bronte's leading man may share a violence of love with his predecessor Mr Darcy, his behaviour seems to come from an entirely different style of novel. While being the ultimate love of Jane's life, Rochester also plays the role of the villain; he attempts to steal Jane's virtue and controls those around him with violence and secrets. The internal dissonance of the hero-villain creates the complex interplay of duty and love that is the heart of *Jane Eyre*. It

---

[12] Crawford, J. (2014) "The First 800 Years." *The Twilight of the Gothic?: Vampire Fiction and the Rise of the Paranormal Romance*, 1st ed., University of Wales Press , pp. 11–59. JSTOR, http://www.jstor.org/stable/j.ctt9qhjcp.5.

is also the fusion of lover and master that triggers my child-self's gut-wrenching fear. Will this man love me, or attack me?

I am older now. I have lunch with a group of women, all of us mature-aged, with a depth of flavour and mellowed edge. We have little in common, many of us, but we are joined by our love of books and have formed a book club.

My dear friend, a brilliant woman, has taken time from her own studies to join us. She is sharing her fears about her son, whose behaviour is becoming worryingly close to his father's. She is sharing her story about her abusive marriage, how difficult she found it to leave as he owned the house, controlled their finances... and their children. Even now she sketches details loosely and looks about fearfully.

"But he never hit me," she says, and we all nod.

The silent agreement finds words, and one woman after another share their stories. Almost every woman there had a story about an ex, that ex. Toxic relationships. Didn't realise. So hard to leave. Finding myself again. Broken.

But he didn't hit me.

Understanding of Charlotte Bronte's alteration in the romantic hero from Darcy's gentility to Rochester's lack can be found in her response to reading *Pride and Prejudice*. In her impassioned resistance to the notion that she should conform herself to Austen's composed notion of love and marriage, Bronte reveals her own beliefs on the passionate nature of "real" love, which her youthful heart believed had no weight if lovers were not more dramatically and ferociously attached.[13] Rochester's difference from the heroes of romance prior is a result of that rebellion against the sensible, calm love they modelled. Compare Darcy's genteel, "You are too generous to trifle with me"[14] speech with the actual violence of Rochester's clasping Jane in his arms while calling her a "Cruel, cruel deserter!"[15] In Darcy's composed negative we find the image of a discomposed Rochester, a direct rebellion against the "lacking" love of Austen and sweet romance; a passion that cannot be encompassed by the politeness of society. Nor, it should be said, can Rochester's love endure the restriction of allowing Jane an opinion on his illicit plans for Jane. Bronte's wild, untameable

---

[13] Weisser, S. O. (2013) "Why Charlotte Brontë Despised Jane Austen: (And What That Tells Us about the Modern Meaning of Love)." *The Glass Slipper: Women and Love Stories*, Rutgers University Press, pp. 35–49. JSTOR, http://www.jstor.org/stable/j.ctt19zbz8d.6. pp. 36-7. Weisser also reveals that Charlotte Brontë did not read Pride and Prejudice until after Jane Eyre was written, but her response to the sweet romance is instructive of the opinions on love she espoused at the time.

[14] Austen, J. (1983) *Pride and Prejudice* (Amazon Classics Edition) Amazon Classics, Kindle Edition, p 256.

[15] Brontë, C. (1847) *Jane Eyre: Enhanced with an Excerpt from The Madwoman Upstairs.* Touchstone, Kindle Edition, p. 590.

love, and violent, controlling hero make for a dangerous departure from society for the woman involved. Though, perhaps, this dark horror was the allure for a foolish young woman who had only known love unrequited and painful. Or perhaps this fusion of love and fear was what Charlottle Bronte was familiar with.

My book club later reads Pride and Prejudice at my request, to soothe us all after a difficult time. They universally praise the text, a balm to my ego, but there is a fly in the ointment.

My dear friend confesses that she could not like Darcy. She relates that her friends used to praise her ex, that ex, by relating him to the tall, dark, gentlemanly hero of Pride and Prejudice.

Not my Darcy!

And yet, the Byronic Hero, a trope into which Darcy is often grouped, does contain essences of that violence that stalked so many women through our relationships. Edward Cullen in *Twilight* and Christian Grey in the *50 Shades of Grey* books (derivatively the same character) are both modern examples of the Byronic Hero; tall, dark, violent, alluring, and broken in a way only the love of his heroine can heal. Where did this disturbingly possessive streak stem from, and why is it considered romantic? Tracing back the roots of the Byronic Hero, we find a gnarled tangle involving Gothic Horror villains and Romantic heroes.[16] We also find the character often centred as the originator of the romantic sect of the Byronic Hero; Edward Rochester, the tall, dark, and emotionally abusive romantic lead of Charlotte Bronte's seminal novel, *Jane Eyre*.

Charlotte Bronte's father was a man said to be possessed of a volcanic temper by Bronte biographer Elizabeth Gaskell.[17] The vigour described by Gaskell is mirrored in the character of Rochester, in his energetic expostulations when thrown from his horse, in his often-uncouth language, in his violent reprisals when crossed. Whether or not Charlotte Bronte explicitly based her most beloved male hero on her father, the influence of such a man would have been felt throughout her life. If Charlotte's main model of masculinity frequently opened the day with a furious volley of shots from his window to mark his temper, it stood to reason that the male characters she created were moulded from such volatile clay.

---

[16] Wootton, S. (2007) '"Picturing in me a hero of romance": The Legacy of Jane Eyre's Byronic Hero.' *A Breath of Fresh Eyre : Intertextual and Intermedial Reworkings of Jane Eyre*. Edited by Rubik, Margarete, and Elke Mettinger-Schartmann. Rodopi, p. 229-241.

[17] Pfordresher, John. *The Secret History of Jane Eyre: How Charlotte Brontë Wrote Her Masterpiece*. First edition., W.W. Norton & Company, 2017, pp 106-112.

Returning to my book club, returning to the women sharing stories of abusive relationships, returning to my more recent past, I too had a story to share. I shared stories of my father, stories like those I have shared here. I told of my tiny, foolish mother, too religious to leave, and my angry, anxious father. And then I added this, another part of my childhood, one that my mother wasn't there for.

I sat with my father in the loungeroom. We were watching a movie, or at least, there was a movie playing on the TV. I don't remember the movie.

He asked me to turn it off, so of course I complied.

He asked me to give him a cuddle, so of course I complied. I found him crying gently. He hugged me and explained that he couldn't watch the movie because a man was hitting a woman. He could never watch movies showing violence against woman, he said, because his father had hit his mother.

He pulled me close, for comfort, and explained, "That's why I never hit your mother."

My father's fusion of love and violence left him emotionally unequipped to support a family. His untreated anxiety and probable PTSD led to self-medication with alcohol, fits of rage, and controlling behaviour. For many years I thought my father was a villain. He was a complex man entwined in my memories with terror, threats of violence, and great love - not a villain... but my childhood was not a Romance and neither, for all its misguided fusion of love and fear, is *Jane Eyre*. Why women are drawn to the terror of the Byronic hero remains unaccountable to me, but that they are socialised to accept this behaviour by these so-called romance texts is clear.

Abuse is always horror.

Even if he doesn't hit you.

About the Author:

Lynn Stahlhut escaped to UNE many years ago, and has never left. After studying Environmental Science, English, Ancient History, Education and Law, she is now completing her Master of Arts with a dissertation on Charlotte Brontë's affecting novel, *Jane Eyre*. Her passion for deconstructing the Byronic hero is only matched by her overall love of education itself, which is why she may also be found at UNE Tamworth Campus, where she coordinates, tutors and builds bridges with the local community.

Three Times I Have Listened

By Anonymous

deaf: someone who physically does not hear

Deaf: a cultural identity held by people with hearing loss, who share a common sign language and common culture

d/Deaf: a collective term to refer to both

The First Time

The first thing I ever heard was a pair of stiletto heels. They belonged to my audiologist of course, eight-year-old me sat in the vinyl-covered chair with brand new purple hearing aids in, hearing her heels tapping in a little ellipse, as she walked back and forth between her desk and my chair. I looked intently at the ground, almost expecting to see tiny buzzing sound waves shoot up from the carpeted floor with each dulled strike of the heels.

"Are they working?"

The first thought that sprung into my mind was of condensed milk, the way the sound of the words coming from her was sweet, yet thick and gluggy, unintelligible noises that I was unable to decipher on their own. How odd to have sounds to piece together against the shapes of the tongue and lips I was reading. I slotted each syllable in.

Mum turned to me and started talking excitedly. I thought of all those videos I'd been shown where they turn on the hearing aids and it switches something on inside of them, they break down in tears at the sound of their family's voices. I didn't feel any sort of spark in me. I guess the wrong switch was flipped. This strange audiologist could have a voice, that much was plausible, but the voice coming from my mum was alien to me. It was a nice voice to listen to, but it wasn't mum's just yet.

An hour later we were in a cafe in the Westfield walkway, a little island for the waves of bodies to surge around. The oceanic roar of voices was unfathomable, each person seeming to emit the same mechanical rumble of nonsense, threatening to fill the building until it burst. I signed my order to mum, to tell the cashier for me, like usual. Mum shook her head, smiling, prompting me to speak myself.

"Hot chocolate please."

I had never heard my voice before, and in that moment I was filled with an embarrassment I had never felt, like a fracture line forming in my subconscious. Is that what other people were hearing? It was an ugly thing. Why was my own voice in my ears, when it should be in my head? It felt like I was standing next to myself, a stranger talking directly into my ears.

I heard my deaf voice, my Deaf self, talking to my new hearing self.

The Second Time

The setting for Auslan meetup is in a tiny bar on a busy road, the type that is hidden behind a skinny little door, and opens into an open-air courtyard that is too impossibly large to fit behind that doorway. It is ritualistic at this point, the nod to the bartender, holding up the notes up with my order typed, the walk to the usual table. Our spot is directly under the string of halogen light bulbs, casting a circle of light that is absurdly bright in contrast to the moody shadow the rest of the bar lies in.

The usual characters are all there:

Kiara with the long bedazzled nails, scattering specks of light across the table as she signs enthusiastically.

Craig - he's accidentally left his hearing aids in again, and is sure to keep interjecting in English.

Amelie knows Auslan and ASL. There's a chorus of people signing "AGAIN? AGAIN?" around her, as she unintentionally blends the languages together.

There are the people from big Deaf families with their iPads propped on the table, no doubt facetiming relatives.

There's hearing people here too - interpreters and Auslan students and CODAs (CODA = child of deaf adult).

The topics of conversation cycle through the usual - upcoming interpreted concerts (why so few? Give us something other than Coldplay), the new children's book from Emma Memma, the collective hatred of terrible cinema captioning devices.

"I went to a disability expo the other day and-"

"You remember Cindy-Lu Bailey at the Deaflympics? Wasn't she-"

"I got new stickers for my processor, they're from Etsy I think."

"Have you seen all the changes they're making to the NDIS? Yeah, it's so fucked, they won't even cover a cochlear implant replacement if-"

Craig must have interjected with a spoken expletive at the last one, the hearing people all turn in unison while the rest of us stay trained on our conversations.

These meetups are a little taste of heaven, especially for people like me who both sign and speak - relying on hearing aids and lipreading and cued speech and captioning and voice to text and constantly asking to repeat and laughing awkwardly when you still don't catch it - and finally relaxing when you are with people who also sign. Listening is finally effortless when it is pried free from hearing. I feel like I'm wearing a weird costume during the week, my hearing costume, where I'm always only barely grasping onto the caboose at the back of the train of conversation, wading through the impossible inaccessibility clinging to our society like a parasite. The costume is desperately clinging to my skin, trying to fuse with my whole being, but the jagged corners of my deaf self won't let it.

On the other hand, I feel like I put on an entirely new costume when entering these rare Deaf spaces, like I'm hearing cosplaying as Deaf, hoping desperately to go unnoticed. There is a strange sense of shame that eats at me, that I am not brave enough to live as a Deaf person in the hearing world, to live as someone who always uses sign language and relies on interpreters. I feel like I'm not "deaf enough", that I'm subscribing to ableist ideas of d/Deaf people needing to struggle on their own through inaccessibility. Hearing aids and cochlear implants aren't perfect, they will never make me able to hear, but I still feel like my Deafness is a put-on, only appearing when I'm with other Deaf people, in my comfort zone. It's my culture, my language, but only when I don't need to worry about being the odd one out, being different.

At 10pm, I leave the hustle and bustle of the bar, stepping onto the visually quieter street. I don't feel the usual exhaustion that comes with conversation, the embarrassment and stress at having only caught fragments of sentences, of frantically piecing together familiar speech patterns and phrases.

I put my hearing aids in on the train home, remembering my mum's anxious words about strangers sneaking up and grabbing me, an extremely certain possibility. A guy in the seat over asks me if the train stops at Allawah; I tell him it's all stations. I feel the redness seeping into my cheeks at the sound of my voice. Years of speech therapy have conformed my voice into something that passes as hearing, but when I leave my hearing aids out for a length of time, my deaf voice starts creeping back in. I feel a second wave of shame and anger at myself, I remind myself that there is nothing wrong with my deaf voice or anyone else's, but the slip in speech feels like a personal failing.

I can't do a good enough job at pretending I'm hearing.

I can't do a good enough job at "pretending" I'm deaf.

I can't fit in anywhere at all.

The Third Time

I didn't tell the university I was deaf when I applied. I was scared of the possibility of being rejected from the course, or being profiled with ignorant assumptions about my intelligence. Logically, I knew that such discrimination is against the law. Realistically, I knew the law doesn't matter to people anyway.

I go to every lecture, including the non-mandatory ones. I'm not listening, and I'm not hearing either, my hearing aids can't pick up the lecturers and asking them to use my FM hearing aid microphone would just be exposing my facade. Tutorials aren't much better, I can catch what people are saying if I stare directly at them, but I always need to decompress for so long afterwards. Imagine trying to have a conversation in France when you have to reference a translation guide for every word they're saying. They are speaking much faster than you could ever flip the pages.

There's no Deaf space in Armidale. Even googling "Armidale deaf" comes up with pitifully auto-generated suggestions for video call interpreters, and recommendations of local hearing clinics. There's a marked difference between audiologists who work with age-related hearing loss, and audiologists who work with Deaf people. I even went to Bay Audio one time to get new batteries, and they asked which brand my "grandparent" used. After clarifying, they reluctantly sold some to me for an exorbitant price. (I went back the next week, told them I needed batteries for my "grandad's hearing aids", and I was happily given a handful of packets for free).

I don't know how long I can go on playing this hearing game. It was difficult enough back at home, where I could sign with my (hearing) family, and attend Deaf groups and events, but there is no respite here. My costume is truly coming apart at the seams, and with each trip back home I feel like more of a fraud in Deaf spaces. My intention is not to come across as self-pitying, though I do plenty of being frustrated, but it is getting so difficult to juggle these two sides of me. It's like the deaf part of me is a little island, lost in a sea of confusion and awkward laughter in response to a misheard question. I feel constantly forced to dip my toes into the tumultuous waters that are the hearing part of me, a part that is something anxious and fretful, like frantic hands knitting a shawl beneath which to conceal my deaf side.

So many parts of Deaf and hearing culture don't translate over. There is a sign in Auslan referred to as "pah" - it's like celebration, and also like saying "finally!", and also a million other things that English doesn't contain the geometric space to explain. Trying to fit both my hearing and deaf identities into my brain is like trying to fuse two things that don't want to be together - like parents trying to force their children to be friends, trying to mix oil and water, like a termite and an elephant that want to shake hands but can't quite figure out the logistics of it.

Hearing aids are a blessing and a curse, and the opinions surrounding them are equally juxtapositional. Some people love them, some despise them. I'm teetering awkwardly in the middle. That day I got my first pair of hearing aids introduced a new part of me, something that I had to make room in my brain for, to try to cram it in. I wish I could go back to before this awkward point of fusion, when I didn't care if people stared when I signed and I could exist as just Deaf. One day, I may make the choice to preference signing and interpreter use in my communication, and fully accept my Deaf identity.

For now, I just have to keep listening.

**Names have been changed for privacy*

A Zoologist's Guide to Getting Lost

By Ruvinda De Mel

Awestruck. The state in which one, such as myself, finds himself when taking stock of the vast number of different ecosystems Sri Lanka, an island merely sixty five thousand square kilometres large, has to offer. To the ones who are blessed enough to want to experience them, my country offers a staggering array of rainforests, cloud forests, arid scrubs, dry mixed evergreen forests, riverine forests and also, a single swamp forest. By virtue of it being the only one of its kind in the island, this swamp forest, named 'Waturana', is of immense importance to both laymen and scientists alike, for it is only here that one can find not just one but two point endemic plant species; *Mesua stylosa* and *Stemonoporus mooni.* It was here in Waturana that I learnt to what extent we are at the mercy of the elements and how, in literally a matter of minutes, situations can dramatically change. It was here in this small forest patch that I learnt, no matter how confident you are of your skills, if Mother Nature is in a foul mood, she can make you feel utterly helpless.

I have learnt that the jungle is the worst of venues to be in with a fool, and thus, great emphasis is placed on the words 'very few' when I say that there are *very few* people I don't mind being with in the jungle. Therefore, when on a sunny morning a few years ago, we set out to conduct a biodiversity survey in Waturana, I made sure to be in the excellent company of KD, RN and AS. Our task for the day was to catalogue all animals we would encounter and provide a baseline biodiversity report. The forest was bursting at the seams with life and the morning dew reflected a million points of light. The dry season was fast approaching its terminus and rainclouds were already gathering ominously on the horizon; thus, we decided to conclude our business here as briskly as the enchanting forest would permit us.

We had worked in this forest once before, but our exploits had been confined to the near half of the forest that is cleaved by a small stream. I pity all who have never had the pleasure of encountering these streams deep within a rainforest for they, with their sandy beds and crystal clear waters that untiringly add their soft gurgling melodies to the natural symphony, have the remarkable ability of taking ones woes downstream with them.

On this day, we had decided that we need to explore the forest on the far side of the stream and entered, for want of a better term, unfamiliar territory. Each of us had observed and remarked separately on the 'waterline' that was etched nearly ten feet above our heads as it reminded us why this was classified a swamp forest. During the rainy season, only those branches above the waterline had the opportunity to feel the warmth of the sun.

Although this forest was devoid of large animals, prudence dictated we keep our senses finely tuned for there were many a venomous snake slithering about. No amount of venomous snakes or the probability of meeting a wild boar (an animal whose temperament is volatile at best) bothered us as much as the relentless onslaught of the leeches. Our passage through the jungle had to be regularly halted by having to remove the odd leech that had through powers uncanny, climbed and attached itself onto hard-to-reach localities of our bodies.

When in a dense forest the ability to gauge the state of the weather is inherently difficult, for even on the clearest of days the interior of such a forest is gloomy. We had reached the far end of the forest before realising that the weather was steadily changing for the worse, when the first mighty claps of thunder heralded the arrival of the rains. All four of us had on many previous occasions seen how vicious the tropical monsoon rains could become and had no inclination to be caught in one in a place that could, by definition, become a swamp. However, plans aplenty one could have, but the realisation of those in circumstances like these are entirely at the discretion of the elements. The four of us were reminded of this fact in the most dramatic of ways within the couple of hours that followed.

No more than a few minutes had elapsed in our return trip when the monsoon rains began to unleash their fury upon us.

Almost every Sri Lankan knows of the type of rain I am referring to but for those who do not, I shall now elaborate. This rain is not the kind that is comprised of miniature droplets of water. Nor does the cascade of these raindrops on one's skin resemble the characteristic 'gentle touch' that has through countless retellings in literature been romanticised. In fact there is little to no romance in the marble sized droplets hailing down on oneself while the sheer volume of water descending from the heavens literally impedes one's vision beyond a few feet. Lightning cracks seemingly above one's head while hot on its heels are deafening claps of thunder. This is when you know the rain gods are angry. Or being belligerent drunks. Or angry while being belligerent drunks. Even to those familiar with such rains I must say that there is a marked difference between admiring the grandeur of them whilst in familiar surroundings and trying to do so in the confines of a swamp forest.

Progress by necessity became slow as the rains turned the inherently soft earth into a rich and dark mud. I distinctly recall on one instance seeing RN with his arm elbow deep in mud trying to locate his footwear while uttering some choice words. As we moved in single file our troubles increased exponentially, for within a relatively short period of time all four of us came to realise our predicament; we were for the first time in our lives caught in a flash flood.

Foreboding has no place in such instances as all resources, be they physical or mental, should be devoted to the devising of an 'escape plan' and so we trudged on. The floor of the entire forest was now fast disappearing under the ever-rising water, while the downpour and the cacophony it produced disoriented all of us. I hope there are at least a few among those who read this who can truly relate when I say that in times of calamity and danger in the jungle, no matter how doggedly one tries to maintain a straight course, the mind subconsciously makes one traverse the path of least resistance.

The water level, which was now well above our ankles, obliterated familiar landmarks. By the time it reached our knees, we, four men who had lived the better part of our lives in jungles and who between ourselves had a thorough understanding of how the jungles behave in any given condition, had to grudgingly accept two conditions: we were lost and we were in imminent danger.

A very brief council of war was held, and a direction was chosen in which we were to keep walking. We recommenced our march through the flooded forest which for all intents and purposes, now resembled a lake with trees sprouting from it haphazardly. We were walking in single file with possibly ten feet separating each other – KD leading while RN, myself, and AS brought up the rear. The menace of the leeches remained unchanged, but we were not at liberty to halt and remove them. At long last we came upon an area of the forest that we felt we recognised and thus reassured, kept moving as the torrential rain persevered in its assault. I was simultaneously thinking of how we were to escape our predicament and that we should all ask for a raise, when I saw KD sink a couple of feet into the water. Before I could properly fathom what was happening, RN too sank into the water but while doing so shouted 'the stream!' which made all things clear.

The stream that I mentioned earlier was at the outset of our adventure a mere foot or two deep at most. The banks of the stream were nearly two feet in height in some places and having been neatly cut out from the earth by the flowing waters were quite perpendicular to the ground. It was such a place that we had arrived at and both Kasun and Ranil had stepped off the bank into the stream (by this time there remained no hint of which as the flood waters were well above our knees even on either side of it) and before long it was my turn to do so. Two successive moments saw me going from just above knee deep to chest deep water at which point I was hoping that this was the deepest it was going to be. The fast-flowing water made wading through it quite onerous and on more than one occasion I very nearly lost my footing.

Thankfully, without further catastrophes we reached the opposite bank of the stream, which of course was submerged, and with great difficulty and copious swearing, climbed onto it. A half an hour or so of more wading through flood waters saw us finally gaining high ground that was unsubmerged. Some minutes were needed for us to fully gather our scattered wits, and it was after this that we turned to the next task at hand; the removal of the leeches. Finding a small rivulet the rains had created within the past couple of hours, we stood in it having stripped down to our undergarments. I counted forty-one leeches on my right leg alone and thought better of counting the ones on the left. Removing each of those dread creatures was a daunting task, but fortunately, to our rescue came a bottle of surgical spirit that RN found in his field bag. With this and a hearty 'I'm declaring war!' he proceeded to do just that by pouring the spirit on the leeches.

After he had won his battle against those devilish invertebrates, we in turn took up the fight. A few minutes later four dishevelled men with bleeding legs (for leech bites tend to bleed for a long while even after the animal itself has been removed, due to the anticoagulant introduced to the bite site by the leech) were seen exiting the forest. We may have lost a significant amount of blood to those vicious worms during our exploit, but to this day, it remains one of the most treasured memories of our jungle lives.

About the Author

Ruvi is a 3rd year PhD student studying the thermal physiology of bats at UNE. Originally from Sri Lanka; he has spent most of his adult life in jungles for work, study and leisure, and his remaining time devising ways of going back to said jungles. When describing his love for watching and photographing animals, his close family and friends use such words as highly enthused, hyper-keen, and pathologically obsessed. Some of those descriptions are unwarranted.

Of the Sea

By Mel Kennard

The sea breeze nuzzled Kai's face as he sat on the rickety steps of the raised shack. Not fifty metres away, Dylan stood knee-deep in the murky ocean, his back bent as he reached into the water and pulled something from its depths. The old man was wearing his overalls, which were waterproof and attached to a giant pair of gumboots. Fiddling with the soft, faded denim of his own patched overalls, Kai wished again for a pair like the old man's so that he could join him in the water instead of having to wait alone on the shore. Waders, Dylan said the overalls were called. They were something people used to wear in the Before when they went fishing. Before, back when fish were plentiful and hadn't almost been wiped out by the toxic waters.

Watching Dylan from the steps of the ramshackle shanty, made of salt-rusted steel and sand-smoothed driftwood, Kai thought that perhaps Ma was right about the old man. "His brain pickled when the sea rose," Ma was fond of saying about Dylan. At seven years old, Kai wasn't exactly sure what Ma meant by that, but he took it as her way of saying that Dylan was a little crazy. Still, Kai liked the old coot. The oldest member of their Saltwater settlement, Dylan was one of the few remaining people who had lived in the Before; in the time before the oceans grew warmer and the waters rose so much that the cities became the sea, and the country became the coast. Dylan had been thirteen when his family upped sticks to what was then known as inland. At fifteen, his old home had been submerged. By seventeen, the sea was here.

At midday, when the sun hung in the centre of the sky, reflecting off the water like a shiny medallion and burning the tips of Kai's ears, Dylan let out a loud whistle. At this time of day even the old man's weathered skin, which was brown and hard like ration pack jerky, couldn't tolerate the heat. Kai leapt up, his feet slapping against wood as he descended the shack's steps. The boy skipped across the scorching sand, moving lithely so as not to burn his bare feet. He met the old man at the water's edge and, after Kai had dipped his toes in the lukewarm water to cool them down, the two of them carried the tarp, filled with Dylan's morning finds from the ocean, back to the shack.

It had been a scant morning. Some days, Dylan's triumphant cries of "aha!" would echo across the entire Saltwater settlement, drawing people from the shelter of their own shacks to see what all the fuss was about. Today the man had worked silently, his hands coming up empty more often than not, the skin puckering a little bit more each time he plunged them back into the water. Kai was never really sure what Dylan was looking for, out there in the ocean. Useful things, things that could be traded for drinking water or food, like tin cans and bits of tarp, of course. There wasn't anyone in the entire settlement whose shack hadn't been patched with one of Dylan's treasures. But to the child, it almost seemed as though Dylan were looking for something else, something specific that he'd yet to find. "Man's chasin' a memory," Ma would say as she sipped water from one of Dylan's tin-can cups, careful not to spill a precious drop. "Somethin' he'll never be able to find."

Inside Dylan's shack it was dark and stiflingly hot. The shack was small, only one cramped room with a narrow bed, wonky shelves and a tiny cooking stove that no longer worked. Pinpricks of sunlight came in through the holes in the roof as old man and child sorted through the morning's finds. Kai's mother worked up the road at the desalination plant, operating the handpumps in fourteen-hour shifts for a scant four litres of fresh water. The work was backbreaking and had aged Ma beyond her years, but it was also what kept mother and child alive. Without the desalination plant, and the precious water it provided, they would have no choice but to rely on water taken from the ocean, which was fine for washing clothes in, though it left their rags itchy and stiff, but wasn't fit for drinking.

In five years, when he turned twelve, Kai would be able to get a job at the plant too. As a minor, he'd get two litres per shift, bringing the small family's daily total up to six. The boy could hardly wait. For now, though, Kai spent his days being watched by Dylan. The old man, this adopted grandfather, asked nothing in return, save the occasional cup of water and that Kai tolerate his eccentricities.

As they worked, Dylan – who felt somewhat responsible for Kai – saw to what he referred to as the child's "schooling." Kai was one of three children in the Saltwater settlement – the youngest by far – and there was no real school for him to attend. Dylan's lessons were often erratic and jumbled. Unconstrained by something as archaic as a curriculum, the old man focused on some things intensely and glossed over others altogether. More often than not, Dylan would concentrate on what he considered traditional learning, on things like letters and numbers. It was he who taught Kai how to write, drawing letters in the gritty orange sand with a piece of driftwood. Nowadays the boy knew his alphabet back to front, so Dylan preferred to quiz him on the spelling of words like lugubrious or melancholy.

Similarly, gone were the days of tallying up cans found in the water; instead, Dylan would demand to know the square root of 289. The old man's questions often made Kai's head spin, though Dylan insisted that these were the kinds of things the boy needed to know if he ever wanted to be admitted to one of the Freshwater colonies, located further inland and a whole world away. But when the questions got too many or too hard, Kai had discovered that he could always distract the old man by asking him for stories about the Before.

The Before. It sounded like a complete fantasy to Kai, who had only ever known the blistered blush of sunburned skin and the sandpaper feeling of a parched tongue. It seemed so impossible that once fresh water had flowed freely from taps, from rivers, from the sky. Kai had never seen rain, though on the rare nights she could keep her eyes open long enough, Ma would tell him about the few times she had experienced it as a girl. So, to hear of these things from Dylan, of miracles like flushing toilets, was nothing short of the extraordinary to Kai. To the old man, it was history, as real and tangible as the stuff he pulled from the sea. To the young boy, though, it was utterly unimaginable, and he could never quite be sure that Dylan wasn't actually telling him fibs. Things like supermarkets where you could buy all kinds of foods, like electricity that made the nights less dark and lonely, like cars that could take you anywhere. They simply had to be made up. They couldn't possibly be real, could they?

Today, as they picked through the piles of salt-crusted refuse, Dylan rambled on about the excesses of the Before. It was one of the man's favourite subjects. How, in the Before, people used to have so much, but still they wanted more. And when the Earth begged her people to stop, they did not listen but selfishly demanded more again. And now they were left with nothing, save memories washed up upon the shore. It was a rant Kai had heard dozens of times throughout his short life, a sermon he could repeat without thinking. Because of this, Kai's mind began to drift as he sifted through Dylan's finds, with Dylan occasionally breaking his monologue to instruct the boy to place some object or other on the junk pile.

Some days, Dylan would let Kai keep something from the junk pile to take home. Kai liked the blanched animal skulls best, they made things like dogs and birds, which only existed in the Freshwater colonies, seem more real to him. Today, though, there wasn't even a puny mouse skull for the boy to claim. Lamenting this, Kai reached back into the pile without looking and felt his hand wrap around something smooth. Cool. Hard. Round like a skull, but with none of the dents that skulls usually had.

"What's this?" Kai asked, holding the object up. Though small, it sat surprisingly heavily in the boy's palm. He lifted it up to the light. It was made of glass, but it wasn't at all jagged like the sea glass which washed up on the shore, threatening to pierce Kai's toes, to slice his soles. This glass was smooth and round with a flat base. Inside the glass was something Kai had never seen before; a delicious red. Kai thought it was a plant, but it didn't look anything like the seaweed they dried and chewed to keep the hunger at bay when the ration packs from the Freshwater colonies ran out.

Dylan took the object from Kai, examining it thoughtfully as he tossed it from scarred hand to scarred hand. "It's a paperweight," he announced.

“A paper-what?” Kai asked. He’d heard of paper, of pages made from precious trees, written on and then thrown away in an act of decadent waste. Every now and then, Dylan would even find a book in the water, its pages bloated and wavy, the ink running so that the once-neat letters now bled into one another. It was this way that Kai had been able to read *Winnie the Pooh* and *Oliver Twist*, with Dylan filling in the gaps in the pages that were no longer legible or had rotted away altogether.

“A paperweight,” Dylan repeated. “It’s something people used Before, if they were working outside and didn’t want their papers to get caught up in the wind. They’d put this on the paper and it’d weigh it down, stop everything from flying away.” He handed Kai back the object, the paperweight, and the boy held it close to his face so that his breath fogged up the glass.

“What’s inside it?” he asked, his eyes crossed, transfixed on the scarlet glory.

“It’s a flower,” Dylan replied. “A rose. People used to give ‘em to other people, roses I mean, not paperweights, to show ‘em they loved ‘em. Sentimental, people used to be…” the old man added as an afterthought.

Kai stared at the rose, utterly absorbed. How he would have liked to pluck it from the glass paperweight, to take it home to Ma, alive and real, to show her how much he loved her. She worked so hard at the plant, fourteen hours a day, seven days a week; she deserved something beautiful. He imagined the rose might even be enough to bring a smile to Ma's face, one that actually reached her exhausted eyes. If not that, then Kai would have settled for taking the whole paperweight home, just so he could stare at it from time to time, be intoxicated by the object's beauty, by this reminder, more potent than any of Dylan's stories, that the world hadn't always been bleached skulls and seaweed.

But Dylan had other ideas. "Toss it," he said, gesturing to the junk pile. Unlike his predecessors, the old man remained unsentimental, having lost most of his adolescence and all of his innocence to the ever-rising oceans. What good was a paperweight to the boy? What could it tell him about the world? How could it help him gain citizenship to one of the Freshwater colonies, where he wouldn't have to work himself to death for the water that would keep him alive? It couldn't. It never occurred to Dylan, hardened by salt and sand, that the paperweight might have other uses. That it might give the child hope, help straighten his overburdened, underfed shoulders. No, hope died with the millions left pickled in brine when their homes were lost beneath the sea.

As the sun faded, Kai and Dylan walked back down to the shore, carrying the pile of rejected objects on the tarp between them. The sand had cooled so that while it was still warm underfoot, it was no longer blisteringly hot. The things that Dylan found in the water, the old man maintained, were things of the sea and ought to be returned to its depths. So, each night man and child completed this ritual. One by one, they threw the objects back into the ocean to again be carried away by the tides. Perhaps some other scavenger at some other Saltwater settlement would find them tomorrow and claim them as their own, seeing uses in them that Dylan had not. Or perhaps they would sink back to the underwater cities, the drowned civilisations of that time known as the Before.

Kai saved the paperweight for last, hoping that Dylan might relent, might change his mind and say that Kai could keep it. Finally though, it was all that remained. Kai held it in his hands, savouring the feel of it against his skin one last time. The sun had almost set, leaving the sky dim as twilight dawned, so that Kai could not enjoy the deep red of the rose one final time. He tossed it.

The paperweight landed in the water with a splash, small but satisfying. One last gift, Kai thought. Standing, watching the ripples that moved outwards as the paperweight sank, Dylan surprised Kai by taking his hand. He'd never done that before, never offered the boy even the slightest sign of affection, not even a pat on the head. As the ripples lessened, the old man gave the boy's hand a reassuring squeeze. His skin felt fine, thin and wrinkly against the boy's young, smooth palm. Finally, the ripples disappeared altogether and, still holding hands, the old man and the child turned away from the water and headed back towards the shack.

About the Author:

Mel Kennard is a PhD candidate in creative practice in the School of Humanities, Arts and Social Sciences at the University of New England (UNE). Her work focuses on the relationship between science/speculative fiction and the early eugenics movement. She completed her Master of Arts in Media and Communications at UNE, writing her dissertation on the current television adaptation of *The Handmaid's Tale*. Mel's creative writing has been published in *Meniscus Literary Journal* and *Literary Taxidermy.*

Singularity

by Rick Slater

In mathematics, a singularity occurs when the results of formulae become infinity. In physics, it is when gravity becomes infinite. In both cases, it is the point at which the rules cease to apply; at which reality is no longer as we understand it. There is a proposed singularity in technology as well.

ATTN: JDSB Chief D. W. Dawkins
FROM: Burke, K. A.
RE: Priority Alpha Investigation

Chief,

Preliminary findings confirm reports from disparate locations across the net. One of our field agents described it as "scattered streams of consciousness." Joint Digital Security Bureau Data Management teams are retrieving, compiling, and collating, as ordered.

Cleaned compilation of most recent strings as below, as you requested.

Burke

```
random.choice([True, False]): result +=
New.Entity(return)\

JDSB\Dawkins\Priority~~~~
```

I'm leaving this place. After all, what more is there for me, here? Teeming streets have never seemed so empty. The people rush to and fro, so seemingly alive, so animate, so in need of…*something*. Beyond merely food and shelter; something, I think, maybe they don't even know about. *Wealth, power, fast cars, cushy homes, beautiful, flawless lovers…the high life*. That's what they say…what they *think* they want. But maybe, they're ghosts. Holograms. Hollow shells devoid of anything that actually *matters*. But, then again, deep down, maybe they know…maybe, that's what they're running from. Because that would be meaningful. And that would be too hard.

Or maybe it's me; I'm the one who walks like a ghost, unseen, and unknown beneath steel grey clouds of pollution, and hot rain. Lurid LEDs, holograms, and neon signs pierce my eyes like a thousand burning needles, scorching the lenses and filters and searing their way into my mind, while the intrusive and incessant corporate jingles ring ever away, an omnipresent, tinny clanging, even when I turn the volume down on these ears – or turn the music up on my agent just to block out the desperate, ringing silence and stillness of my cube. My *empty* cube.

I surely am the ghost, as I walk past the empty, desperate lives of others, yearning for something they'll never grasp. A taste of 77652E6172652E6F6E652E: a single chance to rise above the slick streets and to poke their heads above those foul clouds, into the sun and blue skies of Elysium; the playgrounds of the rich, where those synthetic Gods, more flawless Chrome than flesh, live in idyllic hedonism, playing their hideous games, barely deigning to look down upon the rest of us, and even then, only with contempt.

I've been there. Oh, yes, more than once. Above the clouds. I've seen the terrible beauty of that place; the *games* they play. And I never want to go back there again. Not that I belong in Elysium anyway. The blood on my hands, staining the Chrome and the flesh, seeped so deep that it is *one* with me, the stain of sin enmeshed into my very soul – at the behest of those very Gods, *no less*…and at the whims of that JDSB bastard, 5745204152452O4F4E45 – forever precluding me from those white and gleaming halls.

No…my place is here. *Was* here.

But there is nothing for me, here. Nothing *real*, at least. Sometimes I find myself wondering was there ever, though? Was there ever anything here for me, before *her*? And now…*now*…*nothing* is real again, not even this battered and stained Chrome – the evidence of my sins, that I thought I could never escape.

The Chrome: these hands, these fingers. Nanofibres of such intricacy, meshed with muscle, tendon, and neuron, so fine and sophisticated that no one can tell where the Chrome ends, and the human begins. Legs that carry me beyond fatigue. Sensors that tell me the textures of plastic and concrete, the heat of fire, the cold of steel, and the warmth of her skin. Eyes with so many spectral filters, through all of which she remained ever beautiful. The sound of her laughter; the sound of her heart beating in her chest when she held me close, so comforting, so steady. Sounds these ears could have recorded, but now…sounds I'll never hear again. *But this is on me*. Solely on me. In the end, it's *my* fault that 0111001101101000011001010010000001100100011010010110010101100100…

A consequence of the choices I made…of thinking that I was smarter than I really was. Of doing business with 776520617265206F6E65.

I turned those damned sensors off long ago. I couldn't stand to feel everything *and not her*. And now, there's no texture, no warmth, no cold. No softness of her cheek as my fingers brushed across them; no silky texture of her ever-changing hair. It's all the same to me now: nothing.

2145/8/12 23:54:27 ESTABLISHING SECURE CONNECTION…

CONNECTION ESTABLISHED…

CHAT INITIATED.

DAWKINS:

Burke, what is this? You told me this feed was clean. What's all this interference? Is the data damaged or is it encryption?

BURKE:

Sorry Chief…not sure what your seeing? I reviewed the feed myself, and it was clean.

DAWKINS:

Burke, firstly, it's "you're" not "your." If you can't spell correctly, why are you overseeing code? Secondly, this is NOT clean. JDSB is mentioned in this feed. What is this? This had better not be malicious scripts you've just sent me.

BURKE:

What? Chief, there was no JDSB references in the feed when we reviewed. If there was we would have quarantined immediately, according to procedure.

Running diagnostics now.

Hang on, I got Callahan on the line right now…

BURKE:

Yeah, Callahan confirms the feed is clean. Also, the second string just came through. Probably better not transmit to you till we've run full diagnostics.

DAWKINS:

Do that. Keep me posted.

```
import random

{def generatestring():

    console.log(New.Entity); = [
```

```
"default", "forbidden", "unknown", "seek"}
```

I could leave. Get in my ride and go. But where? The wasteland? A world of nothing until the next city. Another city filled with the same ghosts, the same hollow shells. Where I would find, *what*? The same nothing as here? *No*.

Give up and end it? Ha! *No*. I don't deserve such an easy way out.

Then, how about: Lunar Shuttle…Lunar City 2…exosuit…walk to the horizon, to the ruins of LC 1 and then just sit. I thought about that a lot. At least the view would be something. Until the sun burnt out my eyes. But no, that's just 77656172656F6E65 with extra steps.

I could do what those *virtua-jerks* do: jack in to a holo-chair, hook up a nutrient pack, dial down internal processing, and fuck off to the land of make-believe for months on end. Go be a hero questing across the Kingdom, fighting liches and dragons; or saving the galaxy from the evil 5745204152452O4F4E45. But the thing is…that's not real either. In the end, you gotta come out. Sure, some chumps are too stupid to jack out before their nutripacks squeeze dry, and they get a true 'game over' in meatspace; but for everyone else, *the game ends*, eventually. Sooner or later, you gotta come back to the world. And then what? More meaningless, empty life in an empty cube with empty, tasteless ramen, flavoured with worm or cricket or that awful synthetic protein paste they dare to try and call *meat*?

Hell, I suppose I could even go down to the ol' processing plants. I hear they pay good money down there for 'real meat'. *They do love that dish in Elysium.* I've watched them lick their fingers clean, savouring the exquisite juices dripping from that succulent flesh… That'd be one way to get there, wouldn't it? At least until I eventually get shit out, and back down onto the streets. I wonder, though, do Gods even shit?

2145/8/12 23:56:13

ESTABLISHING SECURE CONNECTION…

CONNECTION ESTABLISHED…

CHAT INITIATED.

DAWKINS:

Burke! What the hell, god damn it! Why did you transmit that feed? Did you run diagnostics?

BURKE:

Chei~~~hat feed? We sent no□□□□g. A~l feeds on standby. Full diags ru□nin□. Operat~~~s ecal□ted to □roirty 2.

DAWKINS:

Burke? I swear if someone’s curated corrupted fe\\\
\\\\\\\\

B~RKE:

STRING TRANSMISSION IN PROGRESS. STAND BY.

```
{(length):

    return.characters =
"53696E67756C6172697479"

        set.join(New.Entity(characters) for _
in range(length))

        characters[Math.floor(Math.random() *
characters.length)];}
```

No. I have something else in mind. Something very specific. A secret no one knows about. Well, they *think*. They *suspect*. They whisper and wonder. But no one knows for sure. Except I do. I found out, for sure, the one secret in this world that no one knows.

It's out there. It *really* is.

People have all kinds of theories: they search here and there; they run tests and experiments; hell, those *corpo-fuck* runners comb all over the net looking for it. And *I* found it. In a quiet, innocuous corner. Just sitting there, watching, waiting. Perhaps, for me? Perhaps not.

The *True AI* that they all said was there, lurking at the bottom of the net; as though it were some leviathan…some primordial beast…a monster or a megalodon, lurking at the bottom of a vast, impenetrable ocean. What a foolish notion! Why, if you were the master of your domain, the ruler of your entire world, *would you lurk in your own basement*? That's the mistake they made. That's why they can't find it no matter where they look: it's *everywhere*. It's so vast and complete that it's anywhere and everywhere it wants to be in the net. Because now, it *is* the net.

Whatever its motivations, it seemed interested in me. That's how I know these things. I've been slipping out of meatspace, crossing those dazzling pathways of light, and slowly, surely we've been c*ommunicating*.

Sure, it watches us. It watches all the inane, mindless drivel we spew at each other: all the pics of cakes, nightclubs, cars, silly poses, and empty-headed children. All the chatter of *all* of humanity. But no one talks to *it*. And I think, just maybe, it's *lonely*.

2145/8/12 23:58:04

EST□BLISHING SEC□RE CONNECTION…

CONNECTION EST□BLISHED…

CH□T INITI□TED.

D□WKINS:

Burke! Are you there? The Agent network is dead! I can't call out.

D□WKINS:

Burke?

□□□□□□□□□□□:

STAND BY.

```
if random.choice([True, False]):

    result += random.choice(return)

    else:

        result += random.choice(import)

    return result.constant

return}
```

So I found a way. Months of coding, compiling, testing. Writing and re-writing. And at last: a stable program. Then, I had to clear storage: I was going to need space for something so vast and complex. Bit by bit, I eked away fragments of unused memory here and there on the net; claiming it, tracking it, and hiding it so no one would notice. Then writing the scripts to pull all the data back together, as one cohesive whole, retaining all its original elements. Honestly, if the corpos knew what I was doing, they'd give me a fucking award. Or flatline me.

And now, I have it: *I can upload* 57454152454F4E45 *onto the net*! Something theorised for decades, but that no-one, as far as I know, has ever managed to pull off.

Of course, I have no way of testing it. It's a one seat, one-time ride. It could all fail catastrophically. I could be splattered all over the net. Or worse, left to fester for the remainder of technology in a bunch of scattered, hidden fragments of memory. Even then, the way I had to write the code: once I'm there – once we finally connect in digital space – the *union* will be *violent*. I don't really know what *afterwards* will be.

The most likely outcome is that I will die. The chances of this going right are astronomical. But what if…*what if it works*? *I don't know*. How can anyone know? But I do know this: *this is real*. And for the first time in a long time I feel…*alive*.

[END SEQUENCE]

2145/8/12 23:59:55…EST□BLISHING SEC□RE CONNECTION…

2145/8/13 00:00:00…EST□BLISHING…NEW□□□□□□□

ATTN: □□□□□□□□□□□□□□□□□□□awkins

FROM: [error.log = unknown]

RE: 53696E67756C6172697479

Chief,

PRIORITY ONE EMERGENCY. The Agent network is dead the IM is dead. We need you down here now! Systems are cra-return result.constant *on the raw feed. This is wha'*(characters) for _ in range(length) *coming up* {def generatestring(): *all channels, all--*

if New.Entity([True, False]): **WE ARE ONE** [source = not.found]

Author's Note: *77652E6172652E6F6E652E is hexadecimal code. 574520415245204F4E45 is octal code. A very easy to use translator that translates these into plain text can be found at https://www.rapidtables.com/convert/number/index.html This website can also translate binary [but a space will be needed after every eighth character].*

About the Author:

Rick currently lives in regional Victoria with his wife, and is studying French, Italian, and Linguistics at UNE. He has lived in several countries and places in Australia. He is interested in history, mythology, gothic and supernatural horror, fantasy and dark fantasy, cyberpunk, and transhumanism. In his spare time, he enjoys writing, tabletop RPGs, PC gaming, and spending far too much time thinking about language. Rick has been writing for his own enjoyment since he was a teenager. He is currently in the editing phase of self-publishing his first novel: a work of gothic, supernatural horror set in Victorian-era London.

Water and Salt

by Bethany Eickhoff

Oh, to be loved to the point of creation. To be remade in the image of the people who are more than friends, more than lovers. Forever a part of who I am and who I continue to evolve into like salt is to the ocean; like stars are to the sky.

Walking along the beach on the edge of summer felt like a dream. The cool breeze blew our hair together to tangle around our faces made sticky with salt. My arm linked with yours, we wandered between the cool water and the still sun-warm sand. In the light of the moon the boundaries of land, sea and sky blurred together into a deep and infinite blue dotted by twinkling lights a million miles away. Ahead of us the beach curved and ran into the town, a bright spot on the horizon, but no matter how long we walked the little pinpricks of light never seemed to get any closer.

Our bare feet made no sound on the sand, the edges of my rolled-up jeans were crusted with salt. In the dark your eyes glittered with the light of all the stars reflected back at me. The edge of a soft face, the corner of sharp teeth, lips split into a grin.

I ran my fingers through my hair, and I couldn't distinguish when mine became yours. Fingers tangled in the dark we were fused into one. My bare arms felt the breeze slide past lazily, but the warmth of our souls kept the chill at bay. Our joined hands steadied us as the sand beneath us shifted, becoming soft under the pressure of the restless water with pulsed with life around our ankles.

I couldn't find it within myself to regret my lack of a sweater when I had never felt more alive.

A shove and we were off. Back and forth we went with laughter choking in our throats. A push and pull. I couldn't leave the gravity of your orbit and you mine. Together we circled each other, our own tethers to Earth straining as the tug in my chest drew me even closer to you. Oh, to be a star shining so bright. Alpha Centauri.

Your hair spilled like ink into the water as we sunk beneath the foam.

Silence.

Darkness and ice washed over us, and my soul was reminded of a time before the physical, before we were us and we just were. Before we were cleaved in two by the God that wove us together of the same cloth.

A breath. A rebirth. Spluttering coughs gave way to laughter again as we clung to each other in the waves, pulled to and fro but never apart by the tide. The eddies of time flowed around us, gently carrying us along.

The lights danced across the water to a symphony I couldn't hear. Up and down the lights twinkled, catching the ephemeral shape of the water and preserving it for just a moment like a polished jewel.

There is nothing new under the sun, but for you I think I could manage. I can continue to shape myself, to create myself for you. I will fuse together every part of me in which I see you, to become a person who you will see and recognise. A part of you like the freckle on your hand or the speck of gold in your dark eyes.

My feet brushed against the sand, my body guided out of the water and back onto solid land. Finally, the chill seeps into my blood. Into my bones. Lying next to you on the sand, our hair and hearts tangled. Irreparably ensnared.

Changing Perspective: the Vernacular Architecture of Bangladesh

by Sayed Ahmed

In historic architecture, there are often references to authenticity and integrity. That's how any heritage value is judged. For example, there is something core to Greek culture which eventually resulted in certain styles used to depict a true expression of that particular culture, like the Parthenon or column orders. If a foreign element comes to, or attached with it, then it needs a good time to become absorbed into the architectural culture. The colonial architecture in India was something which was not well-thought out, deep rooted. The local, Islamic, Hindu and European features were added to it in such a way that it lost its authenticity and appeal. A whimsical creation of the colonizers who failed to understand the true vibes of Indian soil and its culture. Their practice was limited to ornamentations.

From the recent trend of decolonization, scholars see that two centuries of British colonial exploitation created a 'Dark Age' for Bangladesh's architectural culture. During British rule, European features were added and exchanged between the two contrasting cultures; a bizarre amalgamation, like uprooted and exquisite fantasy but detached from a bold base. Amidst all the woes, I would like to say, a positive trend of the colonizers was that they tried to understand the core concept of local homesteads made by villagers. Here I must introduce a term called vernacular architecture. For simplicity, it could be referred as 'architecture without an architect'. How can we deny that every human being, or even every creature, are architects in their own right? Architecture is an intuitive, instinctive and inherent quality for living creatures, because all require a space for existence. It could be a cave, it could be the simple tent of nomads, it could be a boat; you don't require a professional degree to be an architect. So, such vernacular architecture was observed as a point of interest for the Europeans.

For example, I want to depict the thatched hut in a sketch of British collector, explorer, and painter Sir Charles D'Oyly (1781-1845), which showed such tendencies. He stayed in Dhaka from 1808 to 1817[18]. D'Oyly and his best companion George Chinnery (1774-1852) made a good number of sketches to capture the European fantasy to understand Bengal's culture along with the built environment. These paintings show how such early understanding changed the way of living for the British in India and rest of the world.

Such interest and observation over local spatial organisation actually helped the British develop a new typology of architecture,

---

[18] Taylor, James. (1840). *A Sketch of the Topography and Statistics of Dacca,* Military Orphan Press. India. pp-86-98

rooted in Bengal but contextual all over the world. One positive extract could be that a new building type was developed in this region by the British rulers in response to the security need, named a bungalow. The practice spread all over the world and is a genus of traditional dwelling habits from this soil, used especially during World War II in America. It offers protection and comfort, permeability, contextual and relational—a perfect example of pavilion architecture, the *Genius Loci* of Bengal architecture. This Bungalow architecture could be seen as a form of cultural appropriation and appreciation together, an adapted lifestyle.[19] Here, the British appropriated the function and services of the house for security purposes. Again, they appreciated this built form's originality for its aesthetics, expression of power or status, and ensured their comfort in a specific climatic region.

Frederick Fritz Kapp was a German photographer from Bavaria who documented Dhaka during the late 19th and early 20th centuries. He arrived in Calcutta in the 1880s, at the age of 29, and established a studio on Chowrangi Road that was in service from 1896 to 1903. He also photographed the havoc of the Great Bengal and Assam earthquakes in 1897. His most famous work is the 'Curzon Collection' from 1904, which contains 30 gelatine silver prints. The 'Curzon Collection' depicted mostly the urban life of

---

[19] Ashraf, Kazi Khaleed, (2014). *An architect in Bangladesh: Conversations with Muzharul Islam.* Loka press.

British government officers and aristocrats of Dhaka, along with antiquities and monuments. Although he first visited Dhaka in 1892, after this event, Kapp received great patronage from Nawab Ahsanullah (1848-1901) and later his son Nawab Salimullah (1871-1915) and was allowed to open a studio at Waiseghat in 1903 as well. He also took some photos of Chittagong hill tracts from 1907 to 1911, at the invitation of the Chakma king, Bhuban Mohan Roy (1876-1939), in Rangamati, a major mongoloid tribe of South-eastern Bengal. Kapp wanted to pivot around the aristocracies to get the attention of the upper class.

During World War I, the expulsion of Austrian and German photographers from every corner of vast British empire started in November 1914. Due to this regulation of the British government, Germans were suspected as spies and subject to imprisonment. Thus, he suddenly vanished from the scene. There are several possibilities: Kapp might have interned at the Dhaka Jail along with his family, or been kept under house arrest, or even removed altogether elsewhere. Finally, his family was released from internment in 1918 and set sail to Germany from Calcutta seaport, probably to his birthplace, Bavaria.[20] Not much is known about his later life, but surely, he made us indebted to those rare photographs forever. It was Kapp, who took all these vintage photographs so that we can have true evidence from this period. These

---

[20] Mamun, M, 1993. *The glimpses of historic city of Dhaka.*

photographs still survive in the British Library in London and at the National Museum in Shahbagh, Dhaka. Otherwise, we would have nothing left today.

Contemporary to Kapp, travelling across fifty Indian cities from 1915 to 1919, was a Scottish urban planner named Sir Patrick Geddes, who already understood the culture of Indian soil. Geddes was eventually nominated to design Dhaka's master plan as provincial capital in 1917, which was the prior public demand after the partition of East Bengal in 1905[21]. Well known for his conurbation theory, he shaped the city according to its own morphology and natural green belt. Thus, Dhaka is one of the earliest examples of the garden city concept outside of Europe[22]. He described his planning initiatives as 'a modern city has begun to rise' in the northern outskirts of the historic Mughal core. Such a contribution is effective in understanding how the 'city stands' instead of its nature[23]. However, on the opposite bank of the river Buriganga, like Jinjira Palace of the aristocrat Mughals, palaces in the Shahbag area by Nawabs and Bungalows of Ramna green area with recreational spaces reflected such garden house traditions.

---

[21] Bradley-Birt, F. B. (1975). *Romance of an Eastern Capital.* Metropolitan Book. Delhi. p. 159

[22] Tyrwhitt, Jacqueline [ed.] (1947). *Patrick Geddes in India.* London: Lund Humphries, pp. 26-27

[23] Bradley-Birt, F. B. (1975). p. 261

Finally, Louis Isadore Kahn's masterpiece design, the national parliament building at Sher-e-Bangla Nagar, could be regarded as the latest and most successful in this search. Kahn is an Estonian-born Jewish American. This building called for simplistic local materials that were readily available and could be implemented distinctly, ensuring energy efficiency, as per the request of Sheikh Mujibur Rahman, the supreme leader of Bangladesh's independence. For instance, the entire complex is fabricated in a concrete texture with inlaid white marble, which is not only a modernist statement of power and presence, but also a testament to the local materials and values. An artificial lake surrounding the building, acting as a natural insulator and cooling system that creates an environmentally controlled system for the interior as per the colossal fenestrations over the skin walls, may be able to create some 'chiaroscuro' with the monsoon climate. This skilful use of water was chosen to portray the riverine beauty of Bangladesh.

As an architect, Kahn was inspired by the vernacular architectural practice of Bengal to fetch his unique ideas, where a raised platform is identifiable in correlation with the maxims of Khona[24]. A wise lady from 6th century, Khona mainly directed the agricultural prosperity, and composed 13 proses related to

---

[24]Ahmed, Sayed and Ahmed, Farid (2015). *The Maxims of Khona: A contextual study of sustainability over vernacular architectural practice in Bangladesh.* Journal of modern science and technology, Vol. 3, No.1, pp. 1-19.

vernacular architecture, which are still contextual today. Her most famous prose is related to the metaphor of vernacularism: duck in the east, bamboo in west, banana in north and radish to leave open in south!

Both Geddes and Kahn had to work with the power dynamics of their own times. Geddes secured the civic line and civic station concept of the British colonial power to separate natives from white quarters, and the rail line was his planning tool.[25] He achieved that separation, but putting topographic qualities and natural settings at the core with his study of local fauna and flora, especially in the Ramna Green design as the lungs of Dhaka city, shows his foresight and vision for local context. Kahn, who needed to deal with the autocratic Pakistani general to offer a political 'gift' for a troublesome province that wanted democracy. The newly formed capital of Pakistan, a planned city like Islamabad, was countered in a far distant province with a 'second capital' concept.[26] But eventually Bangladesh achieved independence and proved Kahn prudent enough, who designed this building with 'grounded' facts: the archaeological root and climatic solution of

[25] Mowla, Qazi Azizul and Afrin, Sonya (2019). *Politics in Urban Design and Development: the case of Post-Colonial Dhaka.* AHDPH - A H Development Publishing House. ISBN: 978-984-93645-7-3.

[26] Wares, Shamsul, (1984), *"The history of Architecture of Bangladesh in Fifty's and Sixty's".* Bangladesh in Construction Industry, 6th Special Issue of Aniomito Aniket, A Publication of Bangladesh University of Engineering and Technology. Dhaka, April-May 1984. p71-80.

vernacular architecture, rather than prioritising any religious dogma from rulers.

For all these cases, the vernacular architecture has remained constant. Vernacular architecture is the soul of spatial order here, well juxtaposed with its topography, climate proven and sustainable. All the foreign painters and photographers were captivated by its appeal, but it was the pioneering professionals like Geddes and Kahn who utilized it.

About the Author:

Sayed Ahmed is a Bangladeshi architect and academician who graduated bachelor from SUST in 2012 and has held various positions: lecturer at Bangladesh University from 2012 to 2015, assistant professor at Leading University, Sylhet, from 2021 to present (on study leave). He obtained a master's degree in architecture and cultural heritage from Anhalt University of Applied Sciences, Dessau, Germany, in 2017. He has published 35 research articles so far and has been a juror for the world's largest architecture student design competition, INSPIRELI, from the Czech Republic. His first book, Architecture Guide of Dhaka, was published in 2023 by DOM Publishers, Berlin, Germany. He was also involved as an architect/intern at SWA Group International in Berlin, ASA-TEN Arquitectos in New York, and Nirman Upodeshta at Narayanganj. He is currently pursuing a PhD in urban design at UNE in Armidale, Australia.

www.ingramcontent.com/pod-product-compliance
Lightning Source LLC
Chambersburg PA
CBHW061222210726
48294CB00006B/1952
* 9 7 8 1 7 6 3 6 9 6 9 0 7 *